ZOEY Gets a Hobby

Tara Garrett

To order additional copies of this book, contact:
Xlibris
844-714-8691
www.Xlibris.com
Orders@Xlibris.com

ISBN: Softcover   978-1-6698-1896-0
          EBook   978-1-6698-1895-3

Print information available on the last page

Rev. date: 04/06/2022

ZOEY Gets a Hobby

"Mommy, what cha' doing?" asked Zoey.

"Reading", replied Mom.

"Reading what?" giggled Zoey.

"A mystery novel" Mom quietly replied.

Mommy you really like to read.

"I sure do Zoey, it's my hobby" smiles Mom.

Your hob...by?

Yes, it's what I do for relaxation.

"Huh?" chuckled Zoey.

"It's what I do for fun" beams Mom.

Dad's hobby is photography.

Zack's is soccer.

Maybe you should get a hobby too Zoey. Zoey giggles. Mom you sure are funny.

I think I will.

All that afternoon, Zoey pondered the things she really enjoyed.

I really like being a ballerina, maybe my hobby should be ballet. As she twirled in her bedroom, imagining herself wearing a purple tutu and tiara.

"No, this isn't it," insisted Zoey.

I'm too dizzy.

Maybe, playing the piano like Molly, as she banged on her imaginary piano.

Or maybe, the violin like Alex, tilting her head to the side, strumming her imaginary strings.

Or softball like Chloe.

The next day at school, Ms. Williams announced a special guest. He wore a white uniform with a black belt. Ms. Williams said that his name is Sensei Brown. He bowed; the class giggled. Zoey thought he must be smart because he had ten patches on his jacket.

Sensei Brown said that he and his wife were the owners of the new Dojo and invited the class to come for a visit. The class cheered.

Zoey couldn't wait to tell her parents about her day and the visit from Sensei.

Sensei Brown had given the class a free visit certificate for Saturday's class.

Saturday finally arrived Zoey was so excited. As they entered the Dojo, Sensei Brown asked each guest to remove their shoes and bow. Zoey and her parents smiled, removed their shoes and bowed.

The demonstration begun, and the class was intrigued. They kicked, yelled, ran, jumped and punched all the things Zoey loved. At the end of the class, Zoey ran to her parents leaped into her dad's arms. I loved it she yells.

I think this is my Hob..by. Mom smiles and agrees
I Think you're right. Karate it shall be!

Printed in the United States
by Baker & Taylor Publisher Services